CW00551253

The Last Plantagenet?

Jennifer C. Wilson

ACKNOWLEDGEMENTS

This is my first foray into self-publishing, so I owe huge thanks to those who encouraged me to get on, finish the manuscript, and get it out in the 'the wild'. Thanks to everyone who encouraged me to finish the manuscript, and to Vanessa Couchman, Alexia Chapman, James Tucker and Deborah Nixon-Carr for their time in reading through the first draft, and helping me shape it into a much better second draft.

Thanks also to Laurence Patterson of Soqoqo Design for the beautiful cover artwork, Victoria Watson of Elementary V. Watson for her support and excellent editing of the final text, and Elizabeth M. Hurst for her help in navigating the Amazon publishing maze!

And new thanks to the members of Ocelot Press, which I'm so excited to be a part of.

CONTENTS

ABOUT THE AUTHOR

Jennifer is a marine biologist by training, who developed an equal passion for history whilst stalking Mary, Queen of Scots of childhood holidays (she has since moved on to Richard III). She completed her BSc and MSc at the University of Hull, and has worked as a marine environmental consultant since graduating.

Enrolling on an adult education workshop on her return to the north-east reignited Jennifer's pastime of creative writing, and she has been filling notebooks ever since. In 2014, Jennifer won the Story Tyne short story competition, which spurred her on to keep working at her longer fiction. Her debut novel Kindred Spirits: Tower of London was published in October 2015, with Kindred Spirits: Royal Mile, released in June 2017, Kindred Spirits: Westminster Abbey in June 2018, and Kindred Spirits: York was released in January 2019.

She is a founder and co-host of the North Tyneside Writers' Circle, and has hosted a number of workshops and events across the area. She lives in Whitley Bay, and is very proud of her approximate two-inch view of the North Sea.

You can find Jennifer on the following social media sites:

Blog:
https://jennifercwilsonwriter.wordpress.com/

Facebook:
https://jennifercwilsonwriter.wordpress.com/

Twitter: https://twitter.com/inkjunkie1984

Instagram:
https://www.instagram.com/jennifercwilsonwriter/

Amazon:
https://www.amazon.co.uk/l/B018UBP1ZO.

2ND JULY 2011, NOTTINGHAM CASTLE

The fireplace hadn't looked like a time-portal. Of all the things flying through Kate's mind as she gazed around the chaos that was the medieval kitchen, that was the one that stood out.

It was meant to be just an ordinary Saturday. A blissful day, enjoying the pounding of hooves cantering around the grounds of Nottingham Castle. Kate had relaxed for once, watching a re-enactment of the Wars of the Roses, celebrating the town's part in King Richard III's fateful final few weeks, as he travelled to Leicester to meet Henry Tudor, and his fate at Bosworth. As an avid fan of the period, it was Kate's perfect Saturday, watching the actors in their armour or fine costumes. She meandered between the stalls, ate her fill of food from the time, and absorbed the atmosphere, enjoying a break from the drudgery of real life. Now, full of roasted chicken and mulled wine, even in the middle of summer, Kate was casually forgetting the accounts she knew she had to settle when she returned to the office on Monday morning. So few of the re-enactments Kate had watched featured Richard III as the hero of their piece, and yet, here he was, taking centre stage, just where he belonged in Kate's opinion. Too many documentaries, plays and other works cast him as an evil, power-grabbing, child-murdering maniac; today, he was just as she had always pictured him – a man doing his best, no worse than any other medieval monarch, who fell foul of Tudor propaganda. Kate had always supported the underdog, she thought as she wandered around the tents, and Richard was certainly that.

But then the rain started. A summer storm, Kate decided, ignoring the gathering clouds for as long as she could, but once the heavens opened, they refused to close, drenching everyone to the skin as they ran for cover. Ducking inside, Kate found herself standing in front of the former kitchen's grand fireplace, flickering away with fake, LED flames, fake meat roasting on fake spits. A clap of thunder made Kate jump, causing her bag to slide off her shoulder and in amongst the 'burning' logs; she leant in to retrieve it, just at the moment the first bolt of lightning struck.

In a heartbeat, the world went black..

"You! Come along now! This is no time to be idle – hurry, now!"

Kate forced herself to focus. She was standing, albeit uncertainly, still in the same kitchen, beside the great fireplace, but now, the flames were a lot more real than they had been minutes earlier. She gradually realised the voice was coming from a young man in front of her, around her age, shouting at her, wearing a smart, colourful livery, emblazoned with the royal crest. A live kitchen demonstration hadn't been part of the day's programme, but whatever was going on, this man seemed real enough, she thought, looking him up and down. As he continued to stand in front of her, so did his anger.

"Now! This bread isn't going to deliver itself!" he barked at her again, pointing to the pewter tray by the side of the fire.

Kate opened her mouth to argue, explain that she wasn't part of the re-enactment, that there had been some sort of mistake, and that she really was just there to watch, not play along. But the man wasn't listening. He was staring at her, clearly waiting for her to do something. She looked around her in confusion; how had health and safety allowed a man to stand, half-naked, as he turned the spit in the flames, fat from the roasting pig flying in all directions? Wait. A half-naked man? Kate found her eyes wandering, then, remembering the liveried servant and keen to avoid another blast of his anger, she picked up the tray he had indicated, and followed him from the room. The pig, and the man, would no doubt still be there on her return; she could return later, if it so took her fancy. She thought back to every re-enactment she had ever attended, and tried to pull herself together; she knew enough to get through whatever situation she had found herself in.

As they rushed up the narrow stairs, trays balanced precariously, Kate tried to understand what could have happened to her. Her first thought was that it was all a dream; that the lightning must have dislodged some masonry, and knocked her out. But this was all too real. The smells were so pungent, the blazing heat of the fire so fierce, and the cloth of her dress... Her dress! In her haste to pick up the tray, Kate hadn't even noticed what she was wearing. Now, she looked down on herself, noting the intricate, albeit relatively shabby lacing on the front of her gown, leading down to the low-heeled clogs on her feet. All her life she had yearned for a dress like this, although, if she were honest, something of higher class than serving clothes would have been nicer. Then a thought stopped her in her tracks. She had been in jeans, t-shirt and ballet pumps at the re-enactment. Who had dressed her up like this? And where were her own clothes? Nervous, and now uncomfortable at the thought of being manhandled when unconscious, Kate looked about her: the lad who had shouted at her earlier, the other 'servants', those in a higher quality of dress that they were encountering as they made their way through the stone passages; any of these people could have done anything to her. The day felt a lot darker than it had started out. For a moment, the thought flitted into her mind that somehow, this really was fifteenth century England, and clearly, Kate's role in this time was that of a serving girl, not a duchess. But still, it couldn't truly be real, could it? Some sort of concussion, or drug-based stupor, brought on by too strong a medication given to her after she had somehow knocked herself out, or injured herself as she ran in from the rain. That was it. Cobbles did get slippery in the rain, after all.

Despite the turmoil in her mind, Kate kept walking and almost collided with the back of the servant as he paused in front of two heavy wooden doors. They had reached the great hall, Kate surmised, and whatever else was going on, the butterflies in Kate's stomach seemed real enough, as did the blades of the guards' swords as they walked up to the huge doors. The two men nodded to Kate's serving partner, who had brought a jug of wine, as they stood aside for the pair to enter.

The room they entered was exactly as Kate had always imagined a medieval great hall should be. They never seemed quite right when recreated in the twenty-first centuries, but this, this was glorious. Candles flickered on every surface, catching the hints of gold, silver and jewels on the well-dressed courtiers, or picking out the vibrant hues of the draft-excluding tapestries. Somebody had put plenty of effort into the décor and costumes yet, there was nobody around to see it. The whole walk from kitchen to hall, Kate had seen only costumed participants, not one member of the public. Why would you go to all this effort, and do such a great job of recreating the period, if you didn't let the public in to see it? It seemed a waste to her.

Then she noticed him.

Kate had always hated the phrase 'skipped a beat', but that's exactly what she was certain her heart did, as she saw who was literally holding court in the centre of the room.

Richard.

King Richard.

King Richard III of England.

And definitely not the actor who had been playing him with such great aplomb earlier. This man's hair, dark, shoulder length, was real, no wig, and he carried himself with a charisma that was hard to fake, how ever good an actor you were. Kate caught snippets of conversation as she walked through the room; either these actors were keeping far more in-character than any other re-enactment she had encountered before, or, more worryingly, she had somehow been transported back in time, and this truly was 1485. Her mind whirled at the notion, but whatever had happened, and however it had come to happen, she had to deal with the here-and-now first, and get this platter of bread safely onto the table the servant was moving towards.

Following in his wake, Kate was suddenly painfully aware of the length of her dress, and the uneven nature of the floor; even the kitten-height heeled clogs, feeling suddenly like stilettos, were too much for her at that moment. She felt dozens of eyes burning into her, half-hoping, half-fearing that they might just include Richard. Risking a glance at the king, Kate almost dropped her tray. His piercing eyes had indeed found hers, forcing her to meet his gaze, even as she felt herself trembling with, what, desire, terror? She couldn't quite tell. The liveried servant nudged her forwards with the jug he was carrying, and she reluctantly tore her eyes away from the king to place her tray on the table in the centre of the room.

As she moved to leave, in two strides, King Richard moved to block her path. "Thank you, we have been awaiting refreshment. But you, you are new?" There was suspicion in his voice, Kate thought, but only natural considering what was happening in the country. Interest lay just beneath the surface, though, she thought.

"Yes, yes, Your Grace," Kate stumbled out, dropping instantly into a low, respectful curtsey in front of him, thanking her lucky stars for the ridiculous number of times she had practised dropping into such a pose in the privacy of her own apartment. Intensely aware of the suggestiveness of her position, even if it was only what was required, she battled her body, desperate not to flush with embarrassment in front of the court.

"Then we shall look forward to your return," Richard continued, a faint smile playing in the curve of his lips, as he nodded to the male servant who instantly stepped forward to offer Kate his hand to lift her from her curtsey. This last from Richard was quieter, almost inaudible to anyone further away, but to Kate, his voice was like silk.

"Your Grace, I am happy to serve you," she stammered in reply, glad for the lad's hand, now practically supporting her as her body threatened to sway.

Richard smiled at her, before turning back to the group of men, accepting a cup of wine from the one closest to him. Overhearing Richard's mumbled message of thanks to him, Kate realised the man was Francis Lovell, Richard's friend since childhood, and one of his most fervent supporters. Unsure of what to do next, Kate was grateful for the lightest of tugs on her hand, pulling her back, away from the king. Mustering as much composure as she was able, she gathered her skirts and walked out of the room. It was only as the door closed behind her that she realised she had turned her back on the king. Mentally flicking through the many history books she had read, Kate tried to recall as much court etiquette as possible, realising she may just have made a critical error. There was nothing else for it; as soon as she was clear of the guards she ran, or rather, trotted, desperately trying not to fall over her own skirts.

"Interesting," the young man commented, without prelude, out of breath as he caught up with her halfway along the passageway back to the kitchens, bringing her to a halt with another grasp at her arm. "He flirted with you. He doesn't do that. We'll have to watch you." He leaned back against the wall, forcing her to pause too, as he caught his breath and she tried to regain composure.

Kate shook her head, instinctively stepping back, hitting the cold wall as she did so. "No, no, he didn't," she said, desperately clinging to the logic of the situation, what little there was. If this truly was 1485, which it was starting to appear to be, Kate had to remember her position. "He is the King of England; I am just the girl who has brought him his wine. On one single occasion. He was being polite to me, that's all."

"I'm sorry to argue, and I don't know why he did it, but he did. He's been different lately. Cannot quite say as to how, but different. It's Tom, by the way. And he was right, wasn't he? You're new? I didn't mean to shout so harshly earlier. It's my first time in charge here, I'm still finding my way around, and it's been what, three weeks now, on and off."

"In charge?"

"Well, in a way. I've been with the king for years, you see, since before he was king, in fact." There was pride in Tom's voice as they started to make their way back towards the kitchen, Kate falling comfortably in step alongside him. "There's no grand title or land, but I always travel with him, making sure things run smoothly as they can."

This time as they walked together, Kate saw the small nods of respect Tom got from the other servants, as well as taking in more of their surroundings. Too late, she realised he was still speaking.

"...I'll make sure you're ready for tonight."

"Tonight?" asked Kate, but Tom had already swung open the doors, and the noise of the kitchen swept away the rest of her question.

***

Back in the great hall, Richard was struggling to keep

7

his mind clear. He had travelled to Nottingham for plenty of reasons, political and personal, but romantic distraction had not been one of them. Quite the opposite, in fact. Since the death of his queen, Anne, he had fought off the instinct and suggestion that he should take a mistress; he hadn't during their marriage, not seriously, so why should he start now? And when he had dared become closer to his niece, however innocently, the rumours had started with a vengeance. His eyes narrowed, despite himself. Those wretched rumours. He wouldn't think of them. His reign had been full of too many lies and rumours to start listening to them now.

Even Tom had dared to hint that perhaps some female company would be good for him; but Tom was far too presumptuous. He may have been a loyal servant for years, but he was still just that: a servant.

So why was he still seeing the face of the new serving girl? He blamed circumstance; if he had been at home, in London, surrounded by a full court, or even the homely surroundings of Middleham, he was sure the girl wouldn't even have warranted a second glance. It was nothing more than being away from the places he knew best, tugging at his heart, making him feel a loneliness which would pass, he was sure. And yet...

"Richard, did you receive any more word from France?" Francis Lovell's voice broke into the king's thoughts and brought him back to the present. Richard pulled himself together, made himself focus on what was being said, but consciously worried that the wine and ale were not being drunk as quickly as he would have liked; he was keen to call for more refreshments as soon as he was able. Realising that there simply wasn't the appetite, and that he could hardly get drunk on his own, he decided a different course of action was called for, and summoned his scribe.

***

For the rest of the afternoon, Kate hovered around the

kitchen, desperate to be present should Richard send for more refreshments; whether what Tom had implied was true or not, even the chance to be in the same room as him again would be worth whatever was going on here. Everyone was frantic around her, preparing for the court's evening meal, but she hardly registered a thing, torn between trying to find some logic in her situation, and just making the best of whatever that situation was. Was this truly 1485? And if so, did Richard III of England really just flirt with her? There was too much danger to consider if this really was where she thought it was, far too many opportunities to find herself in very real trouble should she get something wrong. And yet, despite this, all Kate could think about was the king. His portraits certainly did not do him justice, even if you ignored the Tudors' alterations down the years. Here was no hunchback, no cripple. He was slight in figure, that was true, not much taller than her, but he was no deformed monster, as described by Shakespeare, and 'enhanced' by others as the years progressed, with changed portraits and demonic portrayals. No hint of a withered arm either, from what she had seen. His hair, collar-length, was raven-black, framed his face, and drew attention to those intelligent, penetrating eyes. All her life, Kate had read papers, books and articles about this man, attended lectures and conferences, listened to every possible argument for and against his character, and here she was, waiting for the man himself to call her back to his hall to collect an empty tray.

Finally, Tom was back by her side, a scrap of parchment crumpled in his hand.

"I've got a treat for you," he said, winking, as he took her hand and led her through the rabbit-warren of passageways to the other end of the building, amid the grand apartments of the court. "His Grace has asked that you should be dressed in more appropriate attire for this evening, and so it shall be – you shall have your choice of gowns."

"What? He? What?" stuttered Kate. There had to be a mistake. The King of England surely couldn't be showing any hint of interest in her, a mere serving girl in this time, could he? After a single moment's meeting? There were still plenty of ladies at court here, attending with their husbands; she had seen glimpses of them as she walked back to the kitchens with Tom. All of them far more glamorous in appearance than she, in their rainbow of silk and brocade. As Kate allowed herself to be pulled along the maze of corridors and stairs, her mind was a whirl. If King Richard was interested in her, for whatever reason, what exactly would she do about it? Would she submit to his wishes, if those wishes ended up what she strongly suspected they may be, or would she resist? Her mind was playing catch-up, still trying to work out what was going on. Suddenly, it hit her exactly what month it was; assuming that it was the same month she had left in 2011 (even if she actually had fallen through time, there had to be some logic to it, surely?), then this was July 1485. In a matter of weeks, King Richard III of England would be riding away from here on a journey which would take him to Leicester, and onto Bosworth Field, to meet Henry Tudor in battle. Kate knew how that day would end, even if Richard and his court didn't. She froze at the thought of the men she'd seen earlier, going off into battle, who might or might not return, and those women too, anxiously awaiting news of husbands, brothers, fathers and sons. Kate had read accounts of the battle, she knew how horrific medieval death in battle could be. Surely Richard deserved some happiness, if that was something she was able to provide?

Arriving at their destination, Kate gasped at the number of dark wooden chests stacked up in the room. Tom had already begun looking for the one he was after; in a matter of moments, he was pulling out a dazzling array of satins, silks and brocades.

"But, who do all these belong to? The ladies of the

court?" Kate asked, fingering the fine material and lifting the lid on another chest which she found contained fur-lined cloaks. For the first time in her life, she cursed the rarity of a hot British summer. Yes, it was cruel by the standards of her own time, but endangered animals and their rights didn't exist in the fifteenth century, and what she wouldn't give to try one on, even if only for a minute.

"That's right. This place isn't as big as the London palaces, so we're not really unpacking everything until it's needed. The ladies simply send their servants down to collect whichever gowns they require, one or two at a time. And you, you have your pick of…" He looked again at the gowns, back at Kate then once more at the gowns. "You have your pick of these." With a flourish, he gestured to three of the dresses he had extracted from the chest. "No purple velvet, I'm afraid, not for somebody of your class, but still, you'll be entirely presentable. It has been made clear to me that you are to be a guest at dinner this evening, and that you should be appropriately attired. One of these should do."

Kate closed her eyes for a moment to steady herself; if this was a dream, then it was the best she had ever had, but if it was real, she was about to select a dress in which she would be formally dining with the court of King Richard III. The more time passed, the more Kate believed it was true. She moved over to the selection Tom had picked out for her, holding each outfit up in turn, standing in front of the large mirror he had just uncovered. With a bit of effort, she might just be able to pull this off; her long reddish-brown hair could just about be wrestled into one of the low buns she had seen in portraits from the period, and she might not have any make-up with her, but with a few pinches of her cheeks, she was sure she could put some life into her pale skin. She wasn't sure how fifteenth century people felt about freckles, but she was certain she was pale enough to look as though she didn't spend too much time out in the sun. Yes, she could make herself presentable for court. She chose her gown.

That night, Kate returned to the great hall, now a bustling hive of activity as the nobles finished their meals and prepared for the evening's entertainment. Kate smiled with pride as she looked down at herself. The deep russet of the silk shone out, matched to perfection with black underskirts and neckpiece, embroidered with white threads. Not quite cloth of gold, but then, she had only been in the fifteenth century half a day; promotion from serving girl to lady of the court wasn't bad considering the timeframe. As she walked, the materials rustled against each other, and for a moment, Kate imagined herself as queen of the court, stepping out in front of her nobles, her ladies-in-waiting, her servants, and taking her place amongst the dancers on the arm of her king. Instead, her reality was simply to watch from the side of the room, as the court began to take their positions in a large circle, and the musicians began to tune their instruments. Still, at least she had had time to practise walking in her gown and heels having found the most uneven cobbles in the castle to gain confidence. If this was real, as she continued to suspect it was, she couldn't afford to take a tumble in front of the whole room.

Now, on Tom's arm, Kate felt more confident than she had earlier, leaning on what she hoped was her new friend for company. Apart from when engaged in matters for the king, Tom hadn't left her side since finding her the gown, Kate realised now. It made sense perhaps; if he was that close to Richard, perhaps he was making sure there wasn't anything sinister to her before delivering her to the evening's festivities, which were now beginning to get underway.

King Richard hadn't joined the dancers, Kate noticed from her vantage point. Instead, he had remained seated at the centre of the top table, the other furniture having been pushed out of the way to make room for the court. As the crowds cleared for a moment, his eyes found hers as they had that morning, and the king nodded in recognition, a smile playing on the corners of his lips as he stood and made his way through the court, waving that the others should continue without him. The crowd simply parted as Richard passed by, acknowledging him with nods, bows and curtsies. In a matter of moments, the King of England was at her side, Tom melting away into the background as though he had never been there.

"You must forgive my impertinence; I realise I sent you for a new gown, but had not even asked your name," said Richard, raising her from her curtsey; a much grander affair now she was in a dress to suit the occasion, even one tied with untrained hands.

"It's Kate, Your Grace," Kate managed to reply. "And I thank you for the gown, it is beautiful. I am truly honoured, if a little surprised at your attention." Glancing around her, she saw a few curious looks in their direction, with people wondering who this new girl was, and why the king was paying her such attention. Richard didn't take his eyes off her.

"There is no surprise intended," he said, ignoring the hint of a question at the end of her sentence. "I spend my days with the same people, always the same, and I feel in need of a refreshing change. You would seem to fit that description."

"I do?"

Richard smiled. "You didn't back away earlier, when you delivered the platter; an interesting decision for a serving girl, and a new one at that... You're different."

Kate gasped; he had noticed her error after all. "I forgot, Your Grace, please forgive me. I am new as you say, protocol escaped me."

"It is forgiven – surely the gown would suggest that. I cannot be seen to be fraternising with the servants, after all." Richard held out his hand to her. "Will you accompany me for a walk?"

"If that is what you wish," said Kate, smiling as she accepted his hand. She glanced at Tom, who was loitering in the shadows behind them, and was relieved to see a smile and nod of encouragement. Despite the heat of the evening, Kate shivered as Richard tucked her arm into the crook of his elbow. Two guards went to follow them, but Richard dismissed them. Kate was alone with the king.

For a moment, Kate said nothing, frantically trying to think of which topic of conversation would be safe; what could you say to a man when you felt you knew him better than he knew himself? She had spent so long researching Richard's life, reading and writing thousands of words about him, his friends, his enemies – yet, how could she chat without arousing suspicion? She knew she was far too informed for somebody of her position in this time.

"You are deep in thought, Kate?"

"I have never spoken with a king, Your Grace. I simply do not know what to talk about," Kate replied, happy to be able to reply honestly; the truth was much easier than trying to hide behind lies.

"Do you know of the rumours, surrounding Elizabeth and I?"

Kate's eyes met Richard's. The scandalous suggestion that Richard had seduced his niece, Elizabeth of York, was well-reported yet she had always struggled to believe it. Why he would raise it now was beyond her.

"I try not to listen to gossip – what do you say about them?"

"That they are just that. Rumours. Of no substance. There has been nobody for me since Anne."

"We were all so grieved to hear of her passing. If there is anything I can do..." Kate broke off, not knowing where to go with her sentence. How exactly did you offer condolences to a king?

Richard smiled, amused at her momentary discomfort, a devilish glint in his eye. "Do you think ill of me, acting like this? Sending for you, sending gifts, without even knowing your name?"

"I do not. As I said, I am honoured that you even glanced at me."

"It would have been difficult not to."

They had reached a heavy door, far away from the great hall. From the guards posted there, Kate presumed that behind the door were Richard's private chambers.

"Shall we?" Richard nodded to the guards to open the door then escorted Kate up to his chambers, where two more men-at-arms waited outside. Having let Kate and Richard through, she heard their pikes cross; clearly, they were not to be interrupted.

Without meaning to, Kate glanced around the room then back at the securely-shut doors. Dark wood lined the walls, with rich furnishings all around, including large, comfortable-looking chairs, tapestries hanging by the windows and plenty of gold and silver plate on the tops of chests and cabinets.

"You are in no danger, Kate, whatever they may say of me. I am no tyrant," Richard said, handing her one of the silver cups, filled with a deep red wine. "The rumours they are spreading about me – it is impossible to relax. I have taken to craving the company of close friends and servants, it is easier than being constantly on display with the court."

"Then talk to me, relax with me," Kate said, trying simultaneously not to sound too enthusiastic, while attempting to avoid glancing at the sumptuous-looking four-poster bed which dominated the room. "I am hardly going to go reporting to anybody, and who would believe me if I did? I am nothing but a serving girl – why would the King of England tell me anything?" She took a sip of the wine to steady her nerves and stop herself from rambling further; it was stronger than she was used to, and a warming sensation began to flood through her. Knowing that too much alcohol would cloud any judgement she currently had left, Kate merely let it touch her lips; she

15

wasn't sure how drunken ladies-in-waiting were received at a medieval court, but she doubted the reaction would be positive. She still couldn't believe how quickly she was becoming used to the odd situation she had found herself in, that such thoughts almost felt normal and rational.

Richard hesitated before drinking deeply from his own cup then sank into a chair by the lit fire. The reflection of the flames danced in his dark eyes as he watched them in silence. Finally, as though he had been weighing his options as to whether to speak plainly or not, he looked up at Kate.

"Let me see what happens when I share something; if suddenly the court knows my secrets, I will know who to blame." There was a challenge in his eyes, but Kate held her nerve. Richard continued. "Everyone thinks I should be worrying about Henry Tudor, and I suppose I am giving him due concern, but I refuse to let him dominate my thoughts and my life. I know I can beat him, in a fair fight. Whether it is fair is the point. I don't know who I can truly rely on if it should come to battle. Which it will, I am sure."

"I don't know what to say, Your Grace; I only know what the servants are saying," Kate replied, her mind in turmoil. What if she told him who to trust and who to avoid? Who would stand by him, and who would betray him? The Battle of Bosworth was a defining moment in the history of England, and Britain – and this was her chance to change everything, to give England the Richard III she felt it deserved, without the upstart Tudors dominating for a century, with Henry VIII and his marital misadventures… Too late, she realised she had been too long in replying. Richard's mind had moved on, as he poured himself more wine.

"Enough of Tudor and battles! Tonight, we shall talk of other things. Tell me about you, Kate, how did you find yourself working here? It is a rare thing for somebody so new to rise so swiftly." The questioning wariness had returned to his eyes.

Kate knew she had to pass this test, to avoid being thrown from the castle, or worse, condemned as a spy. "I, um, just lost my father," Kate began her tale, thinking on her feet, shocked at what seemed like genuine interest on Richard's part. "We were a poor family and when he died, with my mother gone years before, I had nothing. But, I had worked here some time ago, briefly, so I came back a few days ago and begged a position in the kitchen. I was very lucky." Luckier still, now she had met him, Kate thought to herself, as she watched him take in her story.

"Indeed," Richard looked at her to continue.

"There's nothing more to tell, I'm afraid," she said, laughing quietly. "I can hardly ask you anything, can I, Your Grace? I feel I am at a disadvantage in this conversation – nothing to tell and nothing to ask!"

He took another gulp of wine. "There is no disadvantage. And you're quite safe, I promise you. I'm not the sort of man to force myself on somebody, if that troubles you?"

"I believe you, Your Grace," replied Kate, rising from the chair she had perched on, and taking a slow walk around the room. "I've never been in a royal bedchamber, everything is so luxurious." Daringly, she stroked the rich fur covering the bed.

"Richard."

"Richard." She nodded, and returned the smile which flashed across Richard's face.

The king rose from his own chair, joining her at the window she had stopped in front of. She glanced sideways at him before they both looked out across the darkening night.

"I arranged a bedchamber for you," said Richard, meeting her eye.

Kate paused, then nodded. "It will certainly be preferable to sleeping on the floor by the fire," she said, casting her mind back to the textbooks she had read. If not for Richard's intervention, she would have been fighting for position when the castle staff retired for the night, lucky to get even a thin, straw-lined mattress to protect her against the cold flagstones.

"I'll fetch for Tom to show you, when you're ready." There was a hint of dismissal in his voice, despite their physical closeness.

"I'll go now if you want to return to the hall?"

Richard turned, leaned back against the window-frame. "There is no rush."

"Well then, we should continue our talking and I shall refresh our drinks." Kate, having finished her wine, fetched the jug from the table and refilled their cups. "It is my job, after all."

It was gone midnight by the time Tom was summoned to Richard's chamber to escort Kate to the small room off the ladies' chambers she had been assigned in a hurry. As the king bid her goodnight, Kate suddenly felt shy. The first-date dilemma flooded her brain; what was the protocol for wishing the King of England a good night's sleep? In the end, Richard took the decision for her. Reaching for her hand, he raised it to his lips in salutation.

"I'll bid you a good night, Kate, but hope to find you on the morrow?"

"It will be my pleasure, Your Grace. Richard."

With a final shared look between Tom and Richard, Kate was escorted to her room. Tiny, indeed, compared to Richard's chamber, but it was more than a girl like Kate in a time like this could ever have hoped for.

"Not bad from nothing to this, is it?" said Tom, fetching a lit taper from the hallway, and lighting two candles on top of a small stool-table next to the pallet bed.

"It is more than I could ever have hoped for," replied Kate, looking around, wondering if she could convince Richard to lend her a tapestry.

"It wouldn't be looked on favourably if you were to gossip about what happened this evening," cautioned

Tom. "He values his privacy, what little of it he's able to get these days. It's a big leap, from kitchen-girl to lady-in-waiting; I hope you are who you say you are? If you are, then you have my friendship but do anything against His Grace, and I shan't move to protect you."

His candour shocked Kate, but it was understandable. "I assure you, I am who I say I am, and hurting His Grace is quite the opposite of what I want. I admire him greatly, I promise you that, and I rather think your friendship is precisely what I need; courtly life is not one I know."

Tom nodded, apparently satisfied by her assurances, for now. "As I said, I serve the king, and if helping you makes him happy, I am at your service too. For now though, I shall leave you – this court rises early." With a final smile, he left, closing the door behind him and not, as Kate was momentarily concerned, locking it.

Alone for the first time since her arrival, she prodded the layered mattresses on the pallet bed, and lowered herself carefully onto the pile of rich woollen blankets which covered them. Finding it more comfortable than she had feared, Kate snuggled down, craving cosiness, despite the warmth of the night.

3RD JULY 1485

Tom arrived in Kate's chamber at first light, with a maid, introduced as Philippa, to help Kate dress. A selection of gowns had been magicked into Kate's chamber before she arrived last night; she had simply missed them in the candlelight. Now, as the sun streamed in, Kate could hardly believe her eyes: such beautiful gowns, and now even her own servant to help dress her in them. It seemed that whatever had happened, if Kate was going to be in 1485 for even a couple of days, she would have to settle into the rhythm of the court's daily life if she was going to successfully navigate things.

"I don't know what to do, Tom. Today, I mean. I could come back down to the kitchens, help you serve the great hall?"

Tom scoffed at her. "Out of the question, not after last night. You've been seen leaving dinner with the king; you cannot simply go back to serving the next morning. Once dressed, we'll get you along to the solar: best place for you, I suspect."

The room was one of the brightest and warmest in the castle, the morning sun flooding the place with natural light, as the limited number of court women began to arrive for the morning. They sat in groups either sewing, talking, or practising their music, having broken their fast in their private chambers. As Kate had feared, the greeting from the other ladies was cool, to say the least. Even in this small group there were factions, and as a newcomer, Kate knew that nobody was completely convinced she could be trusted. Finding herself a spot near a window at the far end of the solar, Kate gathered needle and thread and cast her mind back to the early days of secondary school, and being forced to make a pencil case, an apron, and a host of other things which had gone almost straight into the bin. Trying to remember the stitches, she made an attempt at some cross-stitch, knowing how odd it would look to the other women if she couldn't produce even simple embroidery. Stabbing at the cloth, and trying not to stab herself, Kate aimed, vaguely, for some sort of memento to take with her, assuming she would be able to carry things. Assuming she would even get home. The thought hadn't really struck her last night, but what if this was it for her now? What if there wasn't a way back? Kate shook her head. Whatever might happen in the future, this was where, or when, she was now and she simply had to make the best of what was turning out to be strange but wonderful situation.

Looking around the group, Kate was painfully aware of how much more at ease she had been with the serving girl Tom had sent to help her. Today though at least, thanks to female assistance, rather than hurried male help, she was in the full regalia of a courtier, albeit a lowly one. The stomacher was pulled tight under her gown, forcing her to sit straight, projecting a confidence Kate certainly didn't feel. Philippa, it seemed, had dressed half the ladies of the court, and the gossip had flowed thick and fast. At least now, if anyone spoke to her, Kate would be prepared with enough news to fit in.

Eventually, after an hour of forcing herself to continue

to stab away at her needlework, one of the younger ladies joined her.

"You're new?" The question came with no preamble.

"Yes, just arrived yesterday." Kate felt no need to recount her servant-to-courtier story; she would skip over the servant element for as much as she could get away with.

"People aren't so keen on 'new' at present, that's all. I'm Elizabeth, that's my mother over there," Elizabeth said, pointing out one of the more finely-dressed ladies. "We're loyal to King Richard but there are plenty who aren't. Make sure you know which side you belong to."

There was a hint of threat in Elizabeth's tone, but it sounded more as though she had been rehearsed in such conversation, with other strangers who may have come and gone through court in recent months.

"I am loyal to His Grace," Kate replied firmly. "And it's Kate, by the way."

"We saw him leave the dancing with you; are you his mistress? Is that why he sent for you? Or is he trying again to dispel the rumours?"

"He did indeed send for me, but that has nothing to do with any rumours. I am merely here to provide him with some company, and bring him his wine." Kate prayed for a distraction or a change of topic, unsure how she could keep up this line of questioning. Thankfully, she got her wish, and her new companion was suddenly drawn to the pattern Kate had been stitching into the material.

"That's such a pretty pattern, but so different to what we usually do – who taught you to sew like this?" Elizabeth took the cloth, into which Kate had sewn her initials, set against a backdrop of the only pattern she had ever been able to do free-style: a row of daisies. "We generally prefer more decorative patterns at court. Nothing so… domestic."

"My mother, I suppose; I don't know – it's the only motif I can sew without a pattern." Images of dreaded

Design Technology courses flooded Kate's mind as she lied, picturing the teacher standing over her, time after time, until the poor schoolgirl had finally got the hang of the daisy chain pattern.

"I shall have to copy them; they will look so pretty on my babe's christening gown, when he arrives." Elizabeth put her hand to her stomach, which Kate now saw was indeed bulging under her gown. Here, at last, was safe territory.

"When are you expecting your arrival?" Perhaps not so safe after all; she very nearly followed this with an enquiry as to whether it was a boy or a girl.

"November. He shall be a strong boy, I am sure. And named Richard, after the king."

Kate turned her face aside as she smiled sadly, thinking of the baby Elizabeth would bring into the world in November. If the child was indeed a boy, and to be named after the king, he would be Henry by then. She hoped that Elizabeth would stand strong, keep her first choice, and give the world another Richard. She imagined there were not many born in the final years of the fourteen hundreds.

"Elizabeth! Come here at once!" The younger woman looked up at her mother's sharp instruction.

"She must want something fetching. I hope we will speak again?"

Kate nodded, smiling at the almost plaintive nature of Elizabeth's question; she sensed that her new companion spent a lot of her time at her mother's beck and call, despite her present condition. Still, having one friend amongst the ladies of court would certainly be a bonus, helping Kate integrate; even if she did have the king on her side, he was only one man, and couldn't protect her from the intrigue of the court.

Having avoided further questioning by virtue of her conversation with Elizabeth, Kate took her opportunity and escaped the solar under the pretence of looking for Tom. Kate spent the rest of the day wandering the halls of the castle, desperately soaking up every ounce of memory, experience and 'feeling' she could. At some point, she reasoned, at least part of this would have to find its way into a book, and what better way to make her writing come alive, than to draw on what she was seeing, hearing and feeling in the here and now? The more she strolled, the more Kate realised how lucky she was to have arrived in mid-summer, when the drafts which entered through every window and beneath each door meant she was comfortable at least in the thick layers of material she had been dressed in; such cool air would certainly not have been welcome in colder weather, and she was sure it would be a nightmare in December.

As she made her way through a quiet passageway, Kate became increasingly aware of footsteps behind her. Hearing other people around the place was nothing to concern her, but these seemed to speed up and slow down in time with her own pace, a soft pad of flat shoes, in contrast to the clicking of her low heels. Kate slowed to a snail's pace, practically not moving, and as she'd expected, the footsteps behind her did the same. She spun around, catching a glimpse of a man in plain, brown cloth disappearing down a side-passage Kate had hardly registered as she passed it. Returning to it as quickly as she could, it seemed empty, leading to nowhere of importance. Kate blinked, a sudden feeling of tiredness coming over her; she had been awake since dawn, it was no surprise the day was starting to catch up with her. Forgetting the strange man, she pressed on and made her way to the great hall, hoping to find Tom setting things out for dining.

Finally finding her way into the cavernous space of the hall, bustling with people preparing it for another meal, Kate felt a hand reach for hers, seemingly from nowhere.

"I haven't seen you all day. I trust you haven't been avoiding me?"

"Your Grace!" Kate looked around her. The king had

chosen his moment perfectly, as nobody was looking in their direction. She held his gaze as he raised her hand to his lips as he had done the night before, but this time, there was suggestion in his eyes.

"Will you dine with me this evening? And dance with me?"

"The first, certainly, but the second, I'm afraid I truly do not know any of your courtly dances. I will gladly watch though; perhaps I can learn for another evening?"

He nodded. "Very well. I shall see you at dinner, My Lady." With a bow, Richard was gone, vanished into the passageway he had appeared from, as though he had never been there at all.

Relieved, Kate finally saw Tom entering from the other end of the hall, and hurried over to him. "Tom, I am to join the court for dinner this evening – will you help me?"

Tom shook his head, then smiled the perfect courtier's smile, as though preparing a young lady to become the king's mistress was the only way he could imagine spending his afternoon. "This way. You're going to need a better gown."

That evening, the great hall seemed to glisten even more than it had the night before. Kate, dressed this time in deep green despite herself (much as she hated to admit it, Tudor green did work well on her), felt as though she could melt into the walls, blending into the tapestries which lined the stone. Then she glanced at her wrist, and caught the glint of delicate gold and diamond, shining out from the bracelet Richard had sent to her just before dinner. It was tiny, yes, compared to some of the jewels she saw decorating the other women, but it was hers from him, and that was more than enough. She had been placed at one of the lower-ranking tables to eat, but now, as the court mingled, she moved gradually nearer the top table, where Richard and his closest companions still sat, watching over proceedings. It was everything Kate had ever imagined a medieval banquet to be: the half-light of candles, the rich smells as plate after plate of the finest food in the kingdom was presented, amid the noise of chatter interspersed with music as the musicians prepared themselves for the evening ahead.

Elizabeth smiled at her, beckoning for Kate to join her. The young woman was standing with a group of women, about the same age as the courtier, all dressed in their court finery for dinner. Kate nodded to them each in turn as she was introduced to a flurry of Katherines, Elizabeths and Annes. At least she would always have a good shot at getting their name right, she thought to herself, desperately trying to pinpoint something about each that would help her remember.

"We don't believe you're not his mistress," said one of the Annes, rubies lining her throat.

"Anne," scolded Kate's Elizabeth, "your boldness will get you into trouble. Although I am inclined to agree." She looked directly at Kate. "As someone who is happily and well-married, I wish you luck." She laughed, cradling her bump as the rest of the women smiled at her. It seemed she was indeed happy in her marriage, a rare thing in a society built on strengthening political relationships, rather than the happiness of a couple.

A quick gesture from the doubting Anne stopped the conversation; it seemed the young men of the court were making their way through the crowd, looking to start the evening's dancing. Kate chuckled inwardly as the distinction between married and unmarried become obvious, with those still seeking a husband instantly pulling themselves up to their full height, inclining necks to best display their jewelled wealth, and fluttering their eyelashes in the general direction of the group. The married women smiled graciously, instead choosing to take the opportunity to find their partners, or retire to a bench to watch from the side of the hall.

Kate joined the latter group, observing the mass of

silks and jewels, but made sure she sat where she could watch the king, who was seemingly so at ease with things, so different from how everyone in her own time would have imagined, so soon before Bosworth. But of course, he didn't know Bosworth was coming, not directly, at any rate. None of them did. They knew a battle of some sort was unavoidable, but the idea of Richard losing, for this group, was unimaginable. He was the king, he had been a successful commander before, and no doubt would be again. Kate had watched the court as they gossiped and laughed amongst the small groups which formed, disbanded and reformed over dinner, and now, as the musicians began to play, started to dance. Part of her wanted to scream at them, tell them what was coming, that they needed to prepare, and how best to deal with the battle which was approaching so quickly, but how could she? A serving girl, telling the future? Visions of Joan of Arc flooded her mind, and she forced herself to focus on the moment, and the man sitting at the heart of it all.

Finally, Richard stepped out from behind the great wooden table, and made his way to Kate. As he approached, Kate finally saw the full finery of his outfit; the plush velvet, cut through with soft sheens of silk.

"For you, My Lady," he said, handing her a cup of wine.

Knowing the strength of it now, Kate reached for the water jug and added a splash to lessen any potential ill-effects. Feeling more confident than the night before, she thanked him for the dress and drew him into conversation about his day, still careful not to appear too interested.

"A quiet day. Letters, planning, nothing of great significance. The minutiae of monarchy is something nobody ever tells you about when they hand you a crown. I haven't managed to pick up a sword or visit the tiltyard for days." Richard flexed his arm in a sword-wielding movement, looking like a cricketer warming up to bowl.

"I shall hold that in mind, if anyone should ever offer

me one," Kate replied, laughing, before realising how potentially dangerous her words were. Luckily, Richard was also laughing.

"I must join in for at least a couple of dances this evening and I do hope you change your mind and join me?" the king asked, gesturing to the dancers who were now moving intricately in a weaving circle.

"If there is something slow and easy, then I shall do my best, but please do not think ill of me if I step on your foot. Would that count as treason, causing such injury to the king?" Kate tried to sound as though she was joking, but the thought did cross her mind. Richard simply smiled, and took her hand.

Feeling in a dream-world, Kate let Richard guide her into the centre of the group as a different dance began and couples arranged themselves opposite each other in two lines. Looking around, Kate wondered who was who in this group of men; she had not been introduced to any of them, but the great and the apparently-good must all be gathered here. All the names from the history books which lined her shelves were suddenly very real. Positioned half-way down the line, Kate had the chance to watch the intricate steps, and once her turn arrived, found herself just about able to follow the general pattern, if not the exact footwork of the dance. As the music came to an end, she dropped into a low curtsey, copying the other ladies, and as Richard once again took her hand, excused herself from a second attempt.

"I fear I have already exceeded my expertise, Your Grace; I would take much more pleasure from seeing it done properly by you and a more-suited partner." That at least was true; watching the ladies and gentlemen of court winding in and out of lines and circles would, Kate imagined, be entrancing to watch when it was done correctly.

"As you wish." Richard turned to one of the other ladies, who Kate recognised from the solar as a friend of

Elizabeth's mother. Thinking she had won a battle, however small, the older woman inclined her head to the king in gracious acceptance, before smirking over her shoulder at Kate and joining Richard in the middle of the room. Kate laughed to herself; life in the fifteenth century really wasn't that different after all.

After three more dances, Richard extricated himself from the group, leaving his partner in the reliable company of Francis Lovell, the two men sharing a smile as Francis stepped into his friend and king's shoes without missing a single step, much to the lady's annoyance.

"I think I have had my fill of dancing for this evening; shall we leave them to their music?" Richard asked, offering Kate his elbow, and nodding that the music and dancing should continue in his absence.

Kate accepted gladly, happy for the chance to escape the hall; even as a nobody, she felt so on show, so on display, and craved the privacy of Richard's chambers for more talking, as there had been the night before. This time, as they walked the route to the heavy door, she knew her mind; there was no doubt how she would react if Richard acted the way she anticipated.

In the privacy of his chamber, Richard poured them both a cup of wine, before sinking again into what was clearly his favourite chair in the room.

"How has your first day as a lady of court been?" he asked jovially, as Kate moved a low stool beside his chair and perched on it.

"You will never know what a privilege it is, Sire, truly. I have had the most memorable and remarkable day."

"Well, long may it continue," Richard replied, looking down at her.

Kate returned the smile which flashed across his face, feeling the confidence to place a hand lightly on his knee, ostensibly to steady herself as she drained the final sip of her wine. He reached out, caressing her cheek with his hand, turning her face upwards. Before she knew it, he leaned forward, and claimed her mouth with his. She felt herself respond before she could make any decision, her body reacting instinctively. Cups tumbled to the floor as they rose as one, already entwined, her arms around his neck, his hands finding their way upwards until they tangled her hair. Kate forgot everything she had worried about, as he guided her, still kissing, to the grand royal bed. Releasing him for a moment, she pulled herself up onto the bed, luxuriating in the rich tumble of fur and wool, and finally felt herself relax.

A moment later, Kate froze. Here was an experienced man, King of England, only recently widowed, with at least one serious mistress on record, and she nothing more than a serving maid. What was he expecting? Experience or naivety? Knowledge of the act, or a blood-stained sheet in the morning? He sensed her hesitance and paused, pulling away to look her in the eye.

"Kate?"

"This, this isn't my first time," she said, hesitantly. The honesty made it easier.

"Nor mine," he replied, laughter in his jagged breath as he reached for the ties on his breeches, his hands shaking.

Kate smiled, and tugged at the ties of his shirt, loosening them sufficiently that with one swift move, she could pull it up and over his head. Her hands reached around his back; for a heartbeat, she felt the curvature of his spine beneath his skin. There was a peculiarity there, after all. A moment later, it was forgotten, as he expertly disrobed her. Here was a man who knew what he was doing when it came to removing a fifteenth century gown, whatever the rumours of his loyalty to Queen Anne. Giving in to the coming pleasure, Kate leaned back against the furs, as Richard joined her on the bed.

Fur tickled Kate's nose, pulling her from her crazed dreams about horses, knights and kings. Half-asleep, she pushed it away, angrily admonishing her cat for once again destroying any chance of a weekend's morning lie-in.

"Who is Captain?" A man's voice jolted Kate. In shock, she sat bolt upright, aware that her cat was nowhere to be seen and that the previous evening's activities hadn't been a dream, somehow induced by a flying lance during the reconstruction's jousting competition.

"Um, a cat," she said, still groggy, hoping Richard wouldn't pry as to why a serving girl with practically nothing would have a pet. "From the kitchens," she added, as an after-thought but he was no longer listening.

"I have business to attend to today but I shall come and find you." Richard leaned across the bed as he threw the covers aside, placing a kiss on her forehead.

"I shall look forward to it, Your Grace," Kate replied, smiling up at him. "I shall be in the solar, I expect, sewing again."

"Sewing, gossiping and power-mongering; I know what truly goes on in such rooms."

"You are right, Your Grace," said Kate, startled by his insight into the female world and trying to think of what conversation she could possibly start with Elizabeth and the others today, sure she would end up giving herself away. Suddenly jolted by the opening of the door, Kate watched in horror as the king summoned two men from the outer chamber. She pulled the covers up to her chest as the strangers entered with Tom following them, a tray of bread and meat in his arms for the king to break his fast. The young lad winked at Kate as he spotted her staring. Suddenly flustered, Kate realised that this was not how a king's mistress would act, and, following last night's activities, that was certainly what she was, for the moment at any rate. There was no modern concept of privacy here Kate reminded herself, loosening her grip on the blanket, even if she still kept her dignity covered. Besides, these men wouldn't reveal their master's secrets; they had some of the best jobs at court and were well-kept in the royal household.

After what seemed an eternity, Richard was dressed. He reached down to Kate who was still in the bed, trying to come to terms with the madness of the situation, and planted a gentle kiss on her lips. Instinctively, she put her arms around his neck, pulling him closer, raising herself up before realising what she had done; preventing the king from going about his day's duties.

"Forgive me, I, I…"

"Forgiven – but please be as welcoming later? I will either send for you, or come to you and I assure you, I will be wishing away every moment until I am able to do so." With a final kiss, he was gone.

Only Tom remained. "Quite an impression you've made there, Mistress Kate," he said, bringing her a portion of bread and mug of ale then dropping casually down onto the bed beside her.

"Tom, I have to ask: has he done this before?"

"Not recently, not that I've been aware of. Not that much since Queen Anne, as far as any of us can tell." He helped himself to a torn-off piece of bread from her meal.

"But that's only months."

"No, I mean since he married her."

Kate's mouth dropped open in shock. "Truly? Nobody? No hidden dalliances behind closed doors? No camp followers whilst away at battle?" She knew he had none of the reputation of his brother, but still, no known mistress was a very big deal.

Tom blushed. "No man is a saint but compared to King Edward; there may have been one or two of the ladies who caught his eye, perhaps distracted him for a couple of weeks, but nothing that Her Grace had to worry about. And nothing ever so quick as with you, I have to say."

"It is nothing, I am sure," replied Kate. "After all, with everything that's going on, your thoughts and feelings are always going to be less steady than usual."

"He will defeat Tudor," said Tom, all humour gone from his face for the first time since Kate had met him. "The Usurper won't stand a chance against our rightful King Richard and we'll all be there to support our Master, whatever it takes."

Kate nodded. She believed it of Tom but knew there were plenty who she knew would find it easy to switch sides and support the victorious Tudor when he took the crown.

"Would you go into battle yourself, if it came to it?" Kate tried to sound casual but she felt her chest tighten at the thought of Tom and Richard riding out at Bosworth, side-by-side, whether that would have happened in reality or not.

"Of course," the young man replied, rising from his place on the bed, refreshing her finished cup of ale and drinking from it himself.

Kate watched him, torn between following the 'rules' of time travel she had seen so much of in film and television, and telling Tom everything she possibly could to help him and Richard through what lay ahead. Before she could make up her mind, a pang of pain shot through her head, forcing Kate to close her eyes and losing the opportunity to say anything.

"Come on, up with you – I have a busy day myself and I need to sort these rooms first. Which means you cannot be in them." To make his point, Tom swept the tray away from Kate, indicating her breakfast was finished.

10TH JULY 1485, NOTTINGHAM CASTLE

The evening sky shone a fierce red as Kate watched the sun set from the battlements. She had been counting the days since her arrival in 1485, marking each in the back of a prayer book left on the table of her chamber, folding another page back every morning to mark her time. Eight days so far, eight mornings waking in either the chamber of King Richard or her own small bed.

Having grown accustomed to her strange circumstance, Kate was cautiously starting to enjoy the rhythm of daily life at a medieval royal court. The early mornings, visits to the chapel, the endless messengers to and from London who updated King Richard on the ever-changing situation overseas as Tudor made his way across the continent, trying to build support for the invasion everyone knew was coming. But there was more than that. There were letters from widows, seeking their husband's pensions in his place, requests from royal favour from one town or another, petty disputes between courtiers, all passing across Richard's desk which was set up in his outer chambers. This, interspersed with hunting, dining and dancing; everything Kate could ever have dreamt of had flown by, a whirl of secret assignations and the most intense, immersive history lesson anyone could have imagined.

Tonight though, she had craved peace from the glare of the court. The ladies had just about accepted her presence but the constant attention for somebody terrified of putting a foot wrong had simply become too much for her; she needed some time away from everything and everyone.

"Shepherds' delight," she muttered to herself, wondering if that was a saying yet or whether she was at risk of witchcraft accusations if she started predicting the weather from the colour of the sky. The memory of Edward IV's mother-in-law facing such a threat in just one reign before Richard's sent a shiver down Kate's spine, despite the warmth of the evening. Kate smiled to herself as she listened to the chatter and music spilling out of the great hall, as the day's good hunting was celebrated.

Kate couldn't help wishing her bag had made the journey with her – her mobile phone would be a charm right now. She could be snapping away or recording snippets of conversation until her battery ran out anyway, no chance of a quick charge-up here. After all this, she really would have to get around to writing that novel she'd always planned. Richard III as a romantic lead; quite a turnaround for the Shakespeare devotees. She had plenty of material now, that was for sure. Thoughts flashed through her mind for a time-travel novel – after treading the fine line this last week or so, she had sufficient information for that too.

"Just a shame I won't have the evidence to prove any of it," she said to herself, too late realising it had been out loud instead. She glanced about her quickly – a hint of either witchcraft or madness would no doubt spell the end of her run as the king's favourite. And if she was thrown in prison or, heaven forbid, executed… Kate shook her head, it was too horrific an idea to consider. A slight pain in her forehead reminded her to seek out more water when she retired for the evening. It was the one particular affliction

Kate had endured since arriving, an inclination to headaches. Kate assumed it was simply down to reduced hydration; after all, there was little water consumption with the court sticking mostly to small ale and wine, watering the latter down only a little when imbibing during the day.

The scraping of metal on stone drew her attention to the tower she had climbed up earlier. Instinctively, Kate braced herself against the stone battlements, only relaxing when she recognised the man's frame, sword in place hanging from his belt.

"Richard! You startled me."

"And you had wandered off again – you seem to do it a lot," he replied, reaching her side.

"I like my own company," Kate said, looking out over the skyline.

"Others don't understand, do they? Everyone thinks I should be like my brother, constantly at the heart of every party. Not enough people understand the pleasure of solitude, the peace you can find in it."

They stood in companionable silence, contemplating the setting sun.

"It's a beautiful view: I wish I could see London like this." Kate broke the silence, as the smoke of the Nottingham's fires merged with the low cloud which had begun rolling in.

"You will. When all this is over, I'll be returning to London and I want you by my side."

Kate's heart lurched at Richard's reference to the future. She forced down the rising panic and rested her head on his shoulder, snuggling into his side. She felt him react to her closeness and responded in kind as they crept into the empty guardroom at the top of the tower.

Darkness continued to creep in as Kate watched the clouds flit across the moon, casting longer and longer periods of blackness across the royal bedchamber. She could hear Richard's rhythmic breathing beside her, wondered whether she could risk getting up and moving to the window to look out across the city again. The night before had been calm after their rooftop adventures. Once they had retreated to his chamber, all he had wanted to do was sit and talk. Kate had drunk in every word and fought the urge to ask questions any scholar would have killed to know the answer to: How did he really feel about his brothers? Had he always intended to take the throne? What had happened to his young nephews, the two little boys known to history as the Princes in the Tower – who really had been responsible for their deaths, a crime so frequently assigned to Richard? What if, after all those who had spoken in his defence down the years, it truly had been him?

Instead, they talked as any new couple talked, of hopeful futures and wild ambitions. There would be a second marriage, he confided; he needed another son, after all. But that didn't mean Kate couldn't be by his side.

"There would have to be a title," he had told her. "You could marry, have a proper place at court."

"I could have my own manor house," she had replied. "We could host you on a royal progress and you and I could go on a progress of our own around every room I owned."

"Then I shall make it a palace, give us plenty to explore," Richard had said while stroking her hair, leaning back against the cushions they had piled on the bed.

Now, hours later, Kate still couldn't sleep. There was so much she wanted to say, wanted to ask. She had earned his trust and yet, even then, there remained a limit. Tom's gossip had filled in some gaps, aided by Philippa's chatter but it wasn't enough.

Tomorrow, she thought, tomorrow she would try and build up some courage.

Fate, it seemed, had other ideas.

"It's not good news, but he'll not say what," whispered

Tom to Kate, as they watched Richard reread the message for what seemed the hundredth time before casting it onto his desk in anger.

Kate hung back at the door, watching, unsure whether she would be welcome; she hadn't seen this side of him before. As soon as the note had been delivered that morning, after reading its contents for the first time, Richard's face had darkened with a quiet fury which, if Kate was honest, had scared her momentarily. She had stayed out of his way for the rest of the day, sewing in the solar, but his mood had somehow infected the whole court as they waited to see what the outcome would be. Now, in his chamber, he turned his face to the wall, his back firmly towards her as Tom crept silently past to place a fresh jug of wine on Richard's desk, glancing at the paper. As the young man returned, he shook his head at Kate, gesturing for her to leave.

"He'll be in no mood for company this evening," said Tom, drawing the heavy door into place and nodding for the guards to take up their positions. Richard was not to be disturbed.

At a loss, and not keen to spend the evening continuing to pretend everything was as normal with the other ladies, Kate wandered out into the castle grounds. It was still warm, with plenty of light left in the sun yet, as she strolled towards the thick walls of the gatehouse.

She had hoped the air would clear yet another headache, which had troubled her since she woke that morning but somehow, the further she got from the royal apartments, the worse it got. The sense that somebody was following her made her spin at the sound of a door crashing shut behind her. The resulting flash of pain jolted her, almost causing her to stumble on the cobbles. In her confusion, her foot slipped on metal grating she swore hadn't been there before. As she grasped for something to steady her, a stranger approached, offering his denim-clad arm. Kate pulled away in shock, confused at what was happening, the denim flashing into the dark robes of a monk before vanishing. She sank to the floor, covering her eyes to try and steady herself.

It was dark when Tom finally found her.

"What are you doing out here?" he demanded, pulling her unceremoniously to her feet. "He changed his mind, he's been looking for you. He was worried."

Kate looked around her. No metal grating, no denim, and thankfully no headache. "There, there was a monk?"

"Out here? Well, of course there was – we've had a visit from the town, some matter or other to discuss with the king. Why do you ask?"

"No reason, he, I, I mean, he took me by surprise, it was dark." Aware how little sense she was making, Kate accepted Tom's offered cloak, and let him lead her back to Richard.

Kate was more mindful after that evening, both of Richard and her situation. The headaches, it seemed, meant something more than too much wine, and knowing that only made it worse. Each time Kate felt the pain beginning, she feared this might be the one which took her away from Nottingham, from 1485, from Richard. Of course, she knew there would have to be an end-point but if there was to be a choice, would she have chosen to stay or go? Perhaps having the decision made for her was the best way. This way, all she could do was hope she wouldn't abandon Richard when he needed her most. For every moment she did have in 1485 though, she was determined to make the most of it. The presence of the monk as the pain had reached its worst point was unnerving though and Kate knew it couldn't be a coincidence, thinking back to that first occasion as she walked to the great hall, and the figure following her. She knew how deeply religious the court was, having members of the church around was nothing unusual, but for the two events to be so linked seemed like too big a coincidence. She would add him to the list of things to beware of as she became more attuned to her new surroundings.

Each day of her stay brought new experiences. Some very welcome, like tucking into an array of medieval dishes provided at every meal; others, less so. Even after three weeks in 1485, Kate still hadn't got used to using the small, curtained alcove for her morning ablutions each time she awoke in Richard's chamber. However, even that was significantly better than the chamber-pot that welcomed her whenever she crept back to her own chamber for the privacy; she simply couldn't bring herself to use the 'facilities' anywhere other than in her own or Richard's private quarters. Silly, she knew, but she was a twenty-first century girl and there were some things she simply couldn't bring herself to face. Three weeks in, though, her worst nightmare came to pass; thankfully, in her own bed and not Richard's, having reluctantly but truthfully told him she was feeling too ill to spend the night with him. She looked in horror as Philippa cheerfully presented her with a clutch of rolled up rags. There were some elements of fifteenth century England she was not so keen to encounter.

Retreating to her bed and clutching the hot, blanket-wrapped stone Philippa had provided to her stomach, Kate took the rare opportunity to stop and think about her situation. She really couldn't believe Richard had fallen for her in such a short space of time. Still, medieval life was a precarious thing; there wasn't always the luxury to stop and think about where your affections lay, but better, if you could, to follow them whilst you could. And Richard certainly wasn't sitting and waiting for anything to happen; he was living his life to the full, ruling, hunting and spending each day as the true king he was. They talked for hours, tucked away in the privacy of his great chamber, at the end of each day, with every conversation convincing her even more, if that were possible, that he truly was no

Shakespearian monster. He told her of the battles he had fought over the years, both on the field and in court, alongside and against his brothers, alongside and against his friends.

No wonder he was troubled, she thought, as they sat in the shadow of the battlements one evening, hidden from view of everyone other than the trusted Tom who was standing as casually as he could, kicking his heels against the wall and watching for anyone who might approach and disturb the royal peace.

"You remind me of Meg," he said, breaking the silence.

"Meg?"

"Someone very special. John and Katherine's mother."

Kate stretched out her hand to cover his. John and Katherine. His illegitimate children, and the only two now left to him, following Prince Edward's death. After the first gesture, though, she hesitated. Should she, the serving girl, know of his children? It was a block in her knowledge, a block in everyone's knowledge, come to think of it – nobody had ever conclusively proved who their mother was or details of either child's lives as they grew older. She assumed John must be somewhere close by from what she had read, possibly even with the court itself. She might even have spoken with him but she had no idea where Katherine was, nor Meg, or even who Meg could have been.

"Is she here?" Kate tried to sound casual.

Richard shook his head.

Taking the matter as closed, Kate sank back on the long, cool grass, and looked up at the darkening sky. Maybe she could ask again later, given Richard's willingness to bring up the subject in conversation. She fought down the ridiculous notion of jealousy. How could she be jealous of something which happened years ago, something she shouldn't even be involved in?

"I could always talk to her," Richard's voice startled

Kate. Clearly the topic wasn't closed after all. "Still can, I suppose, about anything. Same with Anne. Same with you." Suddenly serious, he turned and looked her in the eye for the first time in their conversation. "You wouldn't betray me?"

"Betray you? Never. I swear it. I couldn't."

"There are plenty who could."

"I am not one of them."

"But if somebody asked you, what would you do?" He wasn't letting this go.

"I wouldn't tell them a thing. And I would come straight to you." Kate felt the panic rising in her chest. In her happy, relaxed state, had she said or done something wrong after all? Had somebody reported her?

Richard was nodding in response to her statement. "I need to be able to trust people. Especially now. There's a change coming, I fear – I can sense it. And if I have to make some examples of people to show them who is in command then I shall do it."

Kate thought back to Elizabeth's comment about new people and the worries which must constantly trouble Richard. "You can trust me. Absolutely, trust me."

"Then we'll speak no more of it," replied Richard, smiling at her.

A pang of pain seared Kate's forehead as she went to nod in agreement. Out the corner of her eye, a figure in dark robes flickered past briefly shown in the moonlight, then back into shadows. After so many glimpses of him now, she thought was starting to understand him, that he offered some sort of warning, but she wished he would leave her alone. She had seen enough films and read enough books that featured time travel, Kate knew she couldn't do anything to change the future without endangering it.

"It grows cold, Richard, can we go back inside?" Kate asked, already rising to her feet, not waiting for the answer.

"But of course, the court will be wondering what has

become of me." He offered his arm, showing no surprise in her sudden decision, and the pair made their way back to the hall, nodding to Tom as they passed. There was no sign of the monk.

24TH JULY 1485, NOTTINGHAM CASTLE

Staring out of his chamber's window but seeing nothing to fully distract him from his thoughts, a grimace crept across Richard's face as he remembered his last visit to Nottingham, a smiling wife at his side, a healthy son safely ensconced in his own household, with regular updates from his staff. This summer, he was all but alone despite the best efforts of Francis and his other close companions to cheer and distract him. Still, the presence of Kate was proving a soothing and refreshing balm. He re-read the document Tom had delivered to him that morning. A whole fleet, funded by French gold, lined up at Harfleur, waiting now only for a fair wind to send them across the Channel and onto Richard's shores. It wasn't just that he didn't know where Tudor would land, he didn't even know when he would know, such was the mercurial nature of some of his supporters. Even amongst his greatest nobles, Richard couldn't be sure who would rush to send word to their king, or who would delay, keeping the arrival secret for as long as they could risk. In frustration, his mind wandered, thinking how his predecessors would have dealt with the situation: summary executions, more hostages, threatening the country with violence everyone knew they could easily follow through with. There had been enough violence, treachery and death during his reign so far, he didn't want to add more when he could feel they were getting so close to a resolution. The great battle was coming, he could sense it, and he wanted to be ready for it.

Finally, as he saw Francis leading some of the lads of the castle out onto the grass of the inner bailey for weapons training, Richard knew the decision he had been mulling over for days had been made.

"Fetch a scribe to me, I'll be outside," he called to the young page loitering in the doorway before making his way out into the bailey to join his friend and the young soldiers. He was struck by a sudden urge to at least pretend to kill somebody.

Within the hour, his instructions were on their way to London, in the jacket pocket of his best rider, on the fastest horse available. In less than a week, with a fair journey and safe passage, Bishop Russel, Richard's trusted chancellor, would have delivered the Great Seal of England. Whatever happened next, there would be no delays in the king's orders being issued. Richard suspected there would be plenty to send.

Despite the day's flurry of activity, Kate could sense Richard was becoming weary. Weary and wary. That night, as she sat at his feet, she knew she was seeing the real man, not the king, the public façade. For all his calm public exterior, as soon as the doors closed against the world, the pressure was beginning to show.

"I'm just so tired of all this," he said, as she handed him a cup of wine from the tray Tom had brought to them from the kitchens. The three of them were joined by Sir Francis: a secret enclave, the only ones who saw the real Richard Plantagenet, with all his hopes and fears. "I wish I was back in London, or Middleham. Even having brought the bed along, I'm not sleeping well. I never do." This last was muttered; Kate could tell his friends had heard this before.

Kate's mind flashed to the infamous 'bad night' Shakespeare had given Richard before the Battle of Bosworth, filled with the ghosts of his alleged victims. There must be fresh or dried lavender somewhere in the castle, she thought. Maybe there was a chance for a few good nights' sleep before he left and, if she had a word with Tom, Kate was sure the loyal young man would help slip a sachet under Richard's next pillow, wherever that may be. Sensing the men needed to be alone, she kissed Richard on the forehead, making her excuses, and crept back to her chamber, burying herself in the blankets and not sleeping for the rest of the night.

Richard watched Kate leave and turned to his friends the moment the door was closed. "I want more spies sent out – I need to know that I know everything possible, as soon as possible. But no word to anybody else, is that understood?"

Tom and Sir Francis nodded their agreement. They both understood the importance of image to Richard, especially now.

"We will find trustworthy men, we will arrange it," said Sir Francis, casually stabbing at a plate of meat with his knife.

"I am glad that you can, they seem to be in short order," replied Richard, rising and standing by the window.

"The same could be said for women," Sir Francis continued, carefully, watching Richard's back. "Are we completely sure about your new mistress?"

Tom bristled as he saw Richard tense. He looked directly at Sir Francis as he replied on the king's behalf. "There's no evidence of any wrongdoing, Sir Francis, and believe me, I've been watching her."

"You have?" Richard turned back to the room. "Why?"

"Because she was new, and you took a liking to her. No other reason – I would have watched if she had been a duchess, Your Grace, even a princess."

Richard glared at the younger man. "And?"

"Nothing, Sire, nothing at all, as I say. And you know I would have told you at once if I thought we had anything to fear from her."

"I need to trust you two, more than any others – do not let mistrust between yourselves ruin that."

Sir Francis nodded, carving himself a slice of chicken. "I trust Tom, Richard. If he says there is nothing to worry about, then I shall believe him. I do believe him. But I wouldn't have wanted to leave the matter unspoken. Tudor and his cronies are a crafty bunch and it wouldn't be the first time a mistress had been used against a man."

The matter dealt with, the conversation moved on.

The next morning found Kate once again in the solar, sewing alongside Elizabeth as they worked together on a large altar cloth that Elizabeth's mother had decided would give them all a good project to work on whilst they passed the time before returning to London, and the court at large. As relative novices, the two young women had been given a large patch of black to fill in, whilst the older ladies cooed over the intricate patterns at the other end of the fabric. Kate had finally fallen into a relaxed pattern of conversation with Elizabeth; nothing controversial, mainly about the latest hunt outcome, how handsome Elizabeth's husband had looked yesterday - and therefore how handsome their son would inevitably be – as well as how they all looked forward to the return to London's grander palaces. It was here that Kate lost her footing on the path she had followed so carefully since her arrival.

"I know, it would be fascinating to see Westminster before the fire," she said, realising too late that the fire she spoke of wasn't for almost another three centuries.

"Fire? What fire? What do you know of fire?" The fear in Elizabeth's voice was evident, her pitch rising with her panic. "Is the court in danger?"

"What? No, no, there's no fire. I mean, to see Westminster, to see Westminster…" Suddenly it came to her. "In front of the fire. I'm sorry, that's what I meant, 'before' as in 'in front of' – those magnificent fireplaces, so cosy to rest in front of, from what I hear? I've never been." Kate watched her new-found friend as Elizabeth watched her, her head tipped quizzically to one side.

"You mean in the great hall?" Elizabeth asked. "I don't like it, you know, always had a fear of flames. Sorry, you mustn't tell anyone I reacted like that, please? A simple misunderstanding, that's all. My mother thinks I'm an empty-headed idiot for it at my age. But still, it's the heat, and it's so uncontrollable. It's only natural, I'm sure, especially with this little man on his way soon, I've become even more sensitive to it." Elizabeth rested her hand on her stomach, and smiled up at Kate.

"I'll not say a word, I promise," Kate assured her new-found friend, hoping that Elizabeth would return the favour.

Her fears over letting historical facts slip out were the least of Kate's worries, as headaches continued to plague her. They were now always preceded by a glimpse of the monk, just out of proper focus, on the periphery of her vision, and fractions of the future coming back into her life. One morning, wandering down to the gatehouse, she saw a car pulling up outside the gates, vanishing as she blinked twice to try and clear the pain. Another time, making her way through the castle grounds, fencing of the type used to mark out the joust she had been watching in 2011 almost tripped her up, catching on the hem of her gown; she had only avoided falling by grabbing at the guard who had been sent to accompany her.

Kate thought about getting help, to see if there was some sort of pain relief which might ease the symptoms but from what she could remember reading of medieval history, Kate wasn't so sure about letting the doctors of the day provide her with anything. Instead, she kept herself as hydrated as she could, supping the small ale, diluted with water and limited her intake of the red wine. It was a double benefit anyway, ensuring she continued to keep her wits about her. The incident in the solar proved she was never going to be entirely safe, and between an error in Richard's company and the gradual appearance of items from her own time, she needed more than ever to remain in as much control as possible.

10TH AUGUST 1485, NOTTINGHAM CASTLE

At first, the king's words didn't register. It was only when Kate noticed Richard was staring at her, expectantly, that Kate realised he was serious. Serious, and expecting a reply.

"Hunting? Now?"

"Yes, hunting. We depart tomorrow, for Bestwood. I want you to come."

"Well, I mean, of course, if that is what you plan. Yes, I shall come."

Richard was hardly listening, his mind already elsewhere. "The best park in Sherwood Forest for deer – we'll have the finest hunting of the year."

Sherwood Forest? Kate bit her lip to stop either the tears or laughter she felt sure were about to overcome her. Time travel, that was one thing, meeting Richard, quite another, but hunting in Sherwood Forest? This was turning into a joke. Despite knowing fine well that Robin Hood belonged to Richard I, not Richard III, she now pictured herself finding Kevin Costner fighting Alan Rickman over some great injustice. She glanced around her: such scenes could have taken place in this very room, in the heart of Nottingham Castle, if the legends of the outlaw were true. She hadn't let herself think about Robin Hood or the sheriff so far but now it was all she could see. But it certainly wasn't all she could feel. As she let her mind wander briefly to the planned hunting trip, her forehead throbbed.

Richard was still talking about his planned sojourn, his optimism for success obvious. Clearly, tomorrow, they were off to Sherwood.

The rest of his small court were equally optimistic, Kate noticed, as she made her way towards her chamber, followed by two lads heaving a lined wooden crate. How life had changed in her weeks here, she thought. From tongue-tied, travel-twisted serving girl, to the mistress of the king, in need of a crate to carry her belongings, and servants to carry the crate. She still watched her every move, terrified in part that after her small slip-up with Elizabeth, Richard was somehow keeping her dangling on a thread, waiting for her to make another mistake, something big enough for him to arrest her. If that were the case, surely he wouldn't keep inviting her to share his bed? She knew that if Tom suspected anything for even a moment, he wouldn't hesitate to report back to his master. He might be proving a good friend to her, but he was also unswervingly loyal to his king and Kate knew where his priorities would ultimately lie if anything happened. Perhaps Elizabeth had believed her or had simply forgotten her error. Kate thought of her friends back home and their tales of 'baby brain', forgetting the tiny and momentous in equal measure, maybe female biology had worked in her favour. Finding yet another trinket from Richard as she opened the casket in her room, to begin packing, she suspected she would be safe.

13TH AUGUST 1485, BESTWOOD

Richard loved the noise made by the horses' hooves as they thundered after their prey. The stag, a magnificent creature from the passing glimpse before it dashed away, was making good ground but Richard knew something it didn't. Richard's group was only half the people out hunting today; the rest were waiting for the trumpeted command, ready to dive into the fray and divert the targeted beast back towards the king. There would be no escape and there would be roast venison for all the next evening. The blast rang out with perfect timing as the second group, Sir Francis at its head, sprang into action, pushing their horses onwards, directly towards the stag. The animal paused for a moment, before turning back the way it had come, straight into Richard's path. The king hoped it was a sign.

Kate hadn't joined the hunt. As much as she knew the experience would have thrilled her, she knew her limits. Two free riding lessons each summer throughout primary school would not get her through a hunt, especially taking into consideration her headaches. The slow, half-day ride from Nottingham to Bestwood in the first place had been challenge enough. The pain, if it struck whilst she was cantering through woodland, could prove lethal. She had taken to the archery well enough though, thanks to plenty of practise at jousting demonstrations, and the hawking was enjoyable, so she was more than happy to leave the great challenge of deer-hunting to those who knew what they were doing.

Thankfully, that included King Richard.

As his servants brought in the great carcass, Richard dismounted and approached Kate, a smile brightening his whole face. In front of everyone, he pulled Kate into a close embrace, kissing her forehead, eyes and lips in quick succession as she laughed at his exuberance.

"Victory, my sweet, victory!" he exclaimed, pulling back and gesturing to the stag, which was being carried in by two strong servants, tied onto a thick wooden pole.

Kate remembered Henry VIII's gift of a stag to Anne Boleyn during that tempestuous courtship, and knew how much the prize meant, even for a king.

17TH AUGUST 1485, BESTWOOD

Despite the best efforts of the small section of court, Bestwood was not all happiness. A week after their arrival, Kate spotted a messenger arriving at breakneck speed through the gateway, received immediately by the guards and escorted into the building. Knowing it must be important, she hurried to Richard's chambers, arriving as the messenger backed away, his eyes wide at the king's anger. Kate's head was pounding as she paused in the doorway, distracted by a team of suited and aproned people rushing past her, arms full of coffee pots and packets of custard creams. Somebody, some-when, was preparing for something, clearly. She shook her head to clear the image, seeing the monk making his way towards her, and making eye-contact for the first time. Chills raced through her veins as he held her gaze before departing with a respectful nod. Pulling herself together, Kate took in the scene unfolding in front of her.

In the centre of the room, Richard tore the letter and hurled the pieces into the fire, furious at the content, the writer, every citizen of the city of York. He had never been anything but favourable to the city and the city to him in return. But now, in response to his royal summons, there was no promise of men or arms but a request for more information! What more information could they need?

"York!" he exclaimed as he saw Kate. "Of all cities, York asks for more information. Doesn't send a single man, just a boy on a horse! How can I arrange anything if even York doesn't help?"

Kate rushed to the king, pulling him into the nearest chair and, ignoring the pain throbbing behind her eyes, forced him to sit.

"Come, Richard, all will be well. We are all here to help, we will all do what we can." She gestured to Tom, hot on her heels as she had arrived. Now he stepped forward, nodding in agreement and handing a second note to the king. Kate forced herself to listen to the contents, despite the turmoil threatening to overtake her. Bosworth was getting too close now; she had no clue what would happen to her after the 22nd August 1485. Would she be automatically sent back, or rather forward, to 2011, or would she remain in the fifteenth century? If the latter, then what on earth would become of her? What place would there be for the mistress of Richard III in the England of Henry VII? She couldn't think of it. She focused on the conversation going on around her.

"More word, Your Grace. Northumberland is mobilising and Stanley has agreed to send young George to us in his stead. It is all coming together, Sire, the host is gathering."

Richard nodded, calmed by the news of Northumberland's movement. "We will be victorious, when it comes," he said, as much to himself as to Kate and Tom. "We return to Nottingham tomorrow and then onwards, as agreed," he carried on, looking up at his faithful servant. "Go and advise Francis?"

Tom nodded, backing out of the room to find Sir Francis, never far from the king.

Kate didn't leave him for the rest of the afternoon,

even as the room drifted in and out of her vision, replaced bit by bit with visions from her own time, mingled with the toing and froing of activity within Richard's inner circle, making preparations for their next move. Their holiday was over. Bosworth was coming into view over the horizon, even if only to her.

That night, she cradled Richard's head in her lap, constantly fighting her urge to burst into tears. As the final candle threatened to gutter and fail, she lost the battle. Feeling her tears flow into his hair, the king looked up at her and instantly pulled himself up to sit beside her at the head of the bed.

"Come, Kate, all will be well. Tudor will come, the royal army will come, and there will be a battle, yes, but I have won battles before and I shall win this one too. And we will return victorious. I will return victorious. To you. And all our plans of marriages and manors will fall perfectly together with no more upstarts threatening my rule."

He sounded so confident, Kate almost believed him. But she couldn't hold it in any longer. "Just don't do anything rash, Richard, promise me that? Nobody doubts your bravery and skill but just, stay with your men, stay protected, whatever happens? Don't go careering off after…"

Before she could finish, a clap of thunder shattered the stillness of the August night, followed by a snap of lightning which shocked the room into virtual daylight. As Richard shielded his eyes from the light, Kate looked straight ahead at the vision which had appeared in the corner of the room: the monk. Fully visible this time, no half glimpses. He was looking directly at her, shaking his head slowly. She opened her mouth to speak, but found no words. Her body was shaking, hot and cold at the same time, tears flowing freely down her cheeks, although Kate had no awareness that she was crying. It must have only been a matter of seconds before she nodded to the monk, accepting that she mustn't continue in her warning to Richard but it felt a lifetime, frozen in the lightning bolt's glare.

As quickly as the light had arrived, it was gone, plunging the room into darkness. Richard coaxed the dying candle back into light and lit two more on the desk. Even with the limited brightness, Kate could see the monk was nowhere to be seen. Confused at how Kate was suddenly in such a state, Richard returned to the bed and pulled the covers up over them both, shutting out the rest of the world.

18TH AUGUST 1485, BESTWOOD / NOTTINGHAM

The pain in her forehead was worse than ever when Kate woke the next morning. Despite knowing that their time at Bestwood had definitely come to an end, she smiled to herself at the memory of Richard's words the night before – that he would return to her, victorious – then felt the tears well up again as she knew his words would never be fulfilled and that she couldn't even let him know. The room spun as she tried to sit up, reaching for a sip of ale she hoped would steady her. She felt Richard stir in the bed beside her, even as the screech of a siren blasted through her.

"We could just stay here, together, and let everyone else deal with Tudor," he murmured, reaching out for her, still half asleep.

"Could we? Could you?" she replied, leaning back against the pillows, lazily tracing her finger along his exposed arm. "Is that really the man you are?" The question stopped her, frozen to the core. Had she truly just encouraged Richard to go to battle when he, even half asleep and with a smile in his voice, had suggested staying put. "On the other hand, you are the king – send your armies to deal with the petty usurper and we shall greet them in London when they arrive triumphant, with Sir Francis and Tom at their head."

Kate snuggled down under the covers, fighting the screaming pain in her forehead. He moved towards her, but was distracted by the door slamming open. Tom burst in, breathless.

"More reports, Your Grace! My apologies, I knew you would want them at once."

Richard buried his head in Kate's hair. "Is it anything so critical that an hour more will lead to disaster?"

"An hour, My Lord, but then I fear I shall need your full attention," replied Tom, smiling with the confidence that only full trust would allow. "I shall see to it that the others are advised of its contents."

Kate shot Richard a glance. "You should have gone, but," she pulled his face to hers, "I am glad you stayed." If she had him for only an hour more, then she would surely make it count.

True to his word, an hour later, Richard was dressed and making his way to the outer chambers. When he returned, his face was dark.

"I was right, we must indeed leave today. Now."

Kate was already pulling her undergarments on and had called for Philippa to come and help her dress properly. She couldn't say anything, the lump in her throat making speaking impossible. She nodded to Richard and indicated silently to Philippa to speed up the dressing process.

The rest of the morning was spent in almost total silence, the mood amongst the small group of courtiers suddenly changed, darkened by the news. Tudor was on the march and everyone realised the battle they knew had been coming was now merely days away, however much they had hoped something would happen to stop it. The happy band which had set out for a good time's hunting days earlier, returned sombre, painfully aware that once they reached Nottingham, the party would split. The men would depart for, word had it amongst the ladies, Leicester, with the women being left behind, with instructions to await further news then to travel wherever they were next needed. Troubled looks passed between husbands and wives, brothers and sisters, fathers and their children, all uneasy as to what the next days and weeks would bring.

Kate knew her time left with Richard must be reaching its end. As the men gathered up what they needed to move into battle, with servants fleeing back and forth carrying travelling cots, provisions and messages from one end of the castle complex to the other, Richard finally broke free from discussions to find her, knees pulled up to her chest, curled into the great chair in his chamber; his bed having already been dismantled to take to Leicester, the instructions carried out in record time.

"Are you avoiding me?" he said, crouching in front of her.

"Letting you get on with what needs to be done," Kate corrected him, reaching out a hand to stroke his cheek. "There are important plans to be made, and I would never forgive myself for distracting you if anything were to happen."

"Nothing will happen. I promised you that and, as you know, I keep my promises. We'll get you that husband, that manor house and those progress plans, just a matter of weeks away."

Kate smiled at him, forcing down the urge to cry. If he had arrived just half an hour earlier, he would have found her hurriedly dowsing her face with cold water to hide the tears which had flowed since they returned but now, at least, she looked calm and composed. She wanted more than anything to shout that he shouldn't go or that, if he must, not to try and charge down Tudor on his own; to let his soldiers do the worst of the battle, and to lead, for once, from the back. But she knew she couldn't, and she knew, from her weeks with him that even if he promised to follow her wishes, he wouldn't remember it in the heat of battle. This was no armchair general, happy to let his men face the enemy's charge without him. Even the enemy had said that, when he was cut down in his prime.

"We leave within the hour – I must make final preparations," Richard continued, hauling Kate to her feet. "But this, this is the most important."

Kate noticed the guards quietly close the heavy doors and heard the pikes once again fall into place. One hour. That was all she had left.

As she watched Richard and his men ride away from the castle's walls, Kate felt her grasp on 1485 loosening. Even as she waved at Richard's retreating back, she saw cars mingling with the horses, could hear the tinny echo of a loud-speaker over the rumble of cartwheels. Suddenly, she was aware of a man's presence alongside her on the battlements and knew without looking who it would be. Turning slightly, Kate recognised the attire of the monk who had been following her throughout her stay. Now though, there was no sense of fear or dread about him. He nodded in silence to her, showing an odd deference to the woman he had terrified for the last two months. Kate knew she had followed the rules, his rules, seemingly, by not saying anything to Richard, not trying to change anything. She smiled at the monk and nodded in return. Without a backward glance, he made his way to the tower stairway and vanished into the darkness.

Seeking one final glance at Richard, Kate saw the sun catch on his raised arm as he waved her goodbye. She responded in kind then put her hand to the diamond pendant Richard had given her, felt it rub against the ruby of the ring that had accompanied it and selfishly hoped they would travel back with her. Instinctively, she pulled the daisy-patterned handkerchief from her sleeve and removed the pin which secured her hair, wrapping it in the small fragment of cloth. She wanted to keep every last memory of Richard, of her time with him.

The pain increasing by the second, Kate staggered down to the castle's kitchens, convinced somehow that this had started there and so should end there. She stumbled up yellow-lined steps, ducking instinctively, not needing the "please mind your head" sign but jarring her hip on the metal handrail which had not been there on her last visit when she and Richard had gone to acquire more wine, laughing.

Looking around, her eyesight began to blur, as the kitchen staff she had come to recognise started to melt away, replaced by costumed counterfeits, health and safety obvious at every turn. The meat on the spit was fenced in, the great fire fading into nothing but flickering LEDs, the medieval replaced by the modern.

Kate looked down for one last time, to take in the glory of her gown, but already it was gone, replaced by comfortable, but now somehow dowdy jeans.

The darkness enveloped her as she fell.

**

"Are you alright there, love?"

Kate blinked then recoiled from the torch being shone into her eyes. The man in green was looking concerned, rummaging for something in his bag. She tried to sit up but was forced to remain still by the medic.

"Please, please, where are my things?" Tears once again welling up, she cast about for her bag, even in her dazed state, Kate still tried to cling onto her last thoughts of 1485. She put her hand to her forehead, trying to calm the hangover-like grogginess which filled her head. "Please, I, I had a bag? I had, things." The interior of the St John's tent suddenly seemed too clean, too alien. Stretching, she seemed physically alright, yes, but how had this worked; what state had she been left in? She clenched and released her hands, wriggled her back to test her movement – it was strange without the constricting rigidity of the corset she had been so used to. Once again, the medic resisted her attempts at movement.

"All here, pet, don't worry – you'd fallen a little way from your bag but we gathered everything up. Some nice replica jewels you've got on mind. You want to be careful passing out around here with that lot, one or two of the duchesses had their eyes on them…"

As his voice trailed away, Kate sank back onto the hard, medical bed she had been put on. She had managed to bring it all back with her. She fought back the tears, thinking about what Richard had been riding away to the last time she saw him but couldn't help smiling at the knowledge that at least she had something to remember him by, even if nobody else would ever believe a word of it. The gemstone of her gold ring had slipped around to the inside of her hand. As she cradled the ruby, Kate decided that this was for her and her alone. If nobody would believe her, why risk saying anything in the first place? This adventure would remain between her and Richard.

Or so she thought.

SEPTEMBER 2011, LONDON

At first, Kate ignored the nausea, assuming it was some sort of side-effect from the time-travel. It had never specifically been covered in any book or film that she had noticed, but there had to be some effect on the body, travelling five hundred years in a split-second. The other symptoms were less easy to ignore. A fortnight late for her period, she plucked up the courage and took the test: positive. She sank to the cold floor of her bathroom, arms clutched around her stomach, half-hoping to feel the flicker of activity she knew couldn't possibly be there yet.

How on earth was she going to explain this one?

22ND MARCH 2015, LEICESTER

Kate couldn't believe she had managed it. Of all the hundreds of thousands of people who entered their name into the ballot, here she was, in Leicester Cathedral, watching Richard's remains as they were carried in through the great doors, resplendent in his oak coffin. The cortège was now cleared of the hundreds of white roses, the symbol of the House of York that had been thrown onto it throughout the day.

But here she was, watching the grand entrance on the large television screen that had been installed for those members of the congregation too far removed from the centre of the cathedral. Early, as usual, she had managed to get a seat on the front row, near where the final tomb would be positioned but it did mean a significant stretch of the neck was required to see the actual coffin coming in. She made the effort though, for a moment at least, not content with simply seeing it one step removed.

It truly had been him then, after all that effort, all those jokes about the 'king in the car park', when the dig had first started and when the skeleton was first discovered. And Kate truly was here too, waiting for compline to start and for the first of the services for the reburial to begin.

The weekend had been a blur of lectures, walking tour, tears at Bow Bridge and then, this morning, the great reveal, as his coffin was shown to the public for the very first time then carried away in the sleek black hearse as the crowds followed behind. Kate thought back to the morning the gold-rimmed envelope had landed on her doormat; if she believed in spirits, she knew Richard would be pleased to see her successful in the draw. Who knows, he might even have had something to do with it.

Kate smiled as she spotted Richard's nephew of the seventeenth generation, traced impeccably down the female line, from his sister, the closest DNA match they could find. The reporters in the press conference had been so thrilled when the match was announced. And so had she.

As the service got underway, Kate forced herself to focus, not to get distracted by thoughts of the bones which lay in the coffin she could just about see a corner of if she leaned forward far enough without looking ridiculous. She had had plenty of time since her return to the present to think about Richard and her time with him during those all-important final weeks before Bosworth. For now, she needed to be very much in the moment, taking it all in, to add to the journal she had started the day she had returned to 2011. Her plans to publish had been cast aside, beaten by her desire to preserve the memories, the feelings, the adventure of it all. But it was all there, ready to be read and read again, whenever the world got that little bit too dull.

After the service, taking her turn to walk past the coffin, which was scheduled to lie in state for the rest of the week before being placed in the final resting place, a moment of inspiration hit her, the chance to get the one thing she had wished for most during her time in 1485. Turning to the lady she had been talking to before the service, they struck a deal, each taking a photograph of the other with the coffin. It wasn't perfect, but it was as close as Kate would ever get to having a photo of herself with

Richard.

Walking out of the cathedral, Kate thought back to that morning, as she left her son with his grandparents before entering the cathedral for the early-morning service, the way he had been waving up at the statue of Richard she now stood in front of. He had been as good as gold and was now being entertained by his grandparents in their hotel room not five minutes' walk away which, according to legend, was built on the site of the inn the king had stayed at for his final night before travelling to battle. Kate had pulled out all the stops when arranging their weekend away.

Kate smiled at the thought of the experts, getting so excited when they discovered Richard's great-nephew. But they had one thing very wrong: there was a much, much closer DNA link available to them, which would have proved the skeleton was Richard absolutely conclusively. She would have been happy to help, but then, who would possibly have believed her?

The End.

OCELOT PRESS

Thank you for reading this Ocelot Press book. If you enjoyed it, we'd greatly appreciate it if you could take a moment to write a short review on the website where you bought the book, and/or on Goodreads, or recommend it to a friend. Sharing your thoughts helps other readers to choose good books and authors to keep writing.

You might like to try books by other Ocelot Press authors. We cover a range of genres, with a focus on historical fiction (including historical mystery and paranormal), romance and fantasy. To find out more, please don't hesitate to connect with us on:

Website: https://ocelotpress.wordpress.com/
Email: ocelotpress@gmail.com
Twitter: https://twitter.com/ocelotpress
Facebook: https://www.facebook.com/OcelotPress/

THE KINDRED SPIRITS SERIES

If you want to find out more about the Kindred Spirits world, click for details of the ghostly community of the Tower of London, Edinburgh's Royal Mile the glorious Westminster Abbey and now York.

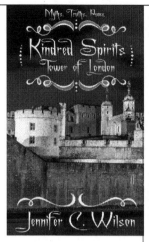

A King, three Queens, a handful of nobles and a host of former courtiers…

In the Tower of London, the dead outnumber the living, with the likes of Tudor Queens Anne Boleyn and Katherine Howard rubbing shoulders with one man who has made his way back from his place of death at Bosworth Field to discover the truth about the disappearance of his famous nephews.

Amidst the chaos of daily life, with political and personal tensions running high, Richard III takes control, as each ghostly resident looks for their own peace in the former palace – where privacy was always a limited luxury.

With so many characters haunting the Tower of London, will they all find the calm they crave? But foremost – will the young Plantagenet Princes join them?

The bestselling Kindred Spirits series continues...

Along Edinburgh's historic Royal Mile, royalty and commoners – living and dead – mingle amongst the museums, cafés and former royal residences. From Castle Hill to Abbey Strand, there is far more going on than meets the eye, as ghosts of every era and background make their home along the Mile.

Returning to the city for her annual visit, Mary, Queen of Scots, is troubled by the lacklustre attitude of her father, King James V of Scotland, and decides to do something about it, with the aid of her spiritual companions. More troubling, though, is the arrival of a constant thorn in her side: her second husband, Lord Darnley.

Can Mary resolve both her own issues and those of her small, ghostly court?

On hallowed ground…

With over three thousand burials and memorials, including seventeen monarchs, life for the ghostly community of Westminster Abbey was never going to be a quiet one. Add in some fiery Tudor tempers, and several centuries-old feuds, and things can only go one way: chaotic.

Against the backdrop of England's most important church, though, it isn't all tempers and tantrums. Poets' Corner hosts poetry battles and writing workshops, and close friendships form across the ages.

With the arrival of Mary Queen of Scots, however, battle ensues. Will Queens Mary I and Elizabeth I ever find their common ground, and lasting peace?

The bestselling Kindred Spirits series continues within the ancient walls of Westminster Abbey.

In the ancient city of York, something sinister is stirring...

What do a highwayman, an infamous traitor, and two hardened soldiers have in common? Centuries of friendship, a duty to the town, and a sense of mischief – until they realise that someone is trying to bring chaos to their home.

Joining forces with local Vikings, the four friends keep an eye on the situation, but then, disaster strikes.

Can peace be restored both inside and out of the city walls?

Printed in Great Britain
by Amazon